Table of Contents

Shark Family Surprise 1

Grandpa Shark's Pirate Crew 17

Little Red Riding Shark 33

Shark Family Bakery 49

The Shark Tooth Fairy 65

Little Fish Lost 81

Love, Baby Shark 95

Grandma Shark's Magic Wand 111

Police Sharks 127

Family Orchestra 143

Balloons and Friends 159

Goodnight, Baby Shark! 175

pinkfong

BABY SHARK™

5- MINUTE STORIES

HARPER

An Imprint of HarperCollinsPublishers

All Stories Adapted by Alexandra West
Design by Elaine Lopez-Levine

Baby Shark: 5-Minute Stories
© Smart Study Co., Ltd. All Rights Reserved. Pinkfong™ and Baby Shark™
are trademarks of Smart Study Co., Ltd., registered or pending rights worldwide.

Manufactured in Italy.

www.harpercollinschildrens.com

Library of Congress Control Number: 2021933212

ISBN 978-0-06-313581-9

21 22 23 24 25 RTLO 10 9 8 7 6 5 4 3 2

❖

First Edition

pinkfong
BABY SHARK™

Shark Family
Surprise

Down deep under the ocean lived a family of sharks. But they weren't your typical sharks. Yes, they had sharp teeth, big fins, and quick tails, but they were the sweetest sharks you could ever meet.

And the sweetest shark of all was named Baby Shark! "Baby Shark, doo-doo-doo-doo-doo-doo!" the little shark sang. "Let's find my family!"

1

When Baby Shark got home, he found Mommy Shark.
"I have a surprise for you, Baby Shark," she said.
"I think it might be waiting for you in the coral reef."
The pair set off toward the coral reef. There were so
many colorful and wonderful things to see in the ocean!

Baby Shark was yellow, and Mommy Shark was a beautiful pink. Baby Shark loved to swim ahead, but he could always spot Mommy Shark's pink fins in the water and find his way back to her.

"Oh, look, I think I see someone we know," Mommy Shark said. "Do you see that blue fin?"

"Blue fin?" Baby Shark said. "That could only mean . . ."

"DADDY SHARK IS HERE!" Daddy Shark boomed. He zoomed through the water and splashed right into Baby Shark. Baby Shark couldn't stop giggling as Daddy Shark pretended to chomp at Baby Shark's tail.

"Are you my surprise?" Baby Shark asked.

"Oh! I almost forgot," Daddy Shark said as he led Baby and Mommy Shark around a big rock. "Surprise!"

Daddy Shark had set up a surprise party *just* for Baby Shark!

"Wow!" Baby Shark said. "Are these cakes and cupcakes all for me?"

"Of course," Mommy Shark said.

Just then Baby Shark began to hear music.

"Baby Shark, doo-doo-doo-doo-doo-doo!" the voice sang.

"Baby Shark, doo-doo-doo-doo-doo-doo! Baby Shark, doo-doo-doo-doo-doo-doo! Baby Shark!" the voice sang.

"Grandma Shark!" Baby Shark said. "I would know that beautiful voice anywhere."

What another wonderful surprise for Baby Shark!

Mommy Shark and Daddy Shark picked up their instruments and began to play along to Grandma Shark's music.

"I thought I would play you your favorite song because you're my favorite grandchild," Grandma Shark said.

"I'm your only grandchild!" giggled Baby Shark.

"The surprises don't end here," Grandma Shark said. Just then Baby Shark heard someone playing the guitar.

"Guitar? I know who that is! Come on!" Baby Shark said as he led his family toward a sunken pirate ship. There they found . . .

"Grandpa Shark!" shouted Baby Shark. The Shark family swam over to join Grandpa Shark as he strummed his guitar. "How did you know where to find me?"

"Oh, Grandpa Shark," Baby Shark giggled. "Everyone knows your secret spot."

"I've never been good at keeping secrets," Grandpa Shark said. "Except my secret recipes! I made all your favorite foods just for your next surprise . . . a picnic!"

After their picnic the Shark family decided to play a game. "Who is ready to play some bubble ball?" Daddy Shark said. "The first shark to catch a big bubble and swim it to the endzone wins!"

"And no cheating this time," Grandma Shark said, looking over at Grandpa Shark. He just laughed. "What! No one said we couldn't pop the bubble!"

Mommy Shark started the game. "On your marks, get set, go!"

Baby Shark was in the lead! He was closing in on a giant bubble when he saw something orange out of the corner of his eye.

"William?" Baby Shark said as he recognized his best friend. "My family and I were just playing bubble ball."

"I LOVE bubble ball!" William said. "Is this part of your surprise picnic? OH NO! I let the secret slip!"

Baby Shark giggled. "You're so silly, William. I already know about the picnic. Now come on, help me get this bubble back to the endzone!"

Baby Shark and William swam back to rejoin his family with the bubble.

"There you are, Baby Shark!" said Daddy Shark. "Looks like you won this game of bubble ball!"

"Woo-hoo! Victory dance!" William said. Baby Shark and William danced and celebrated winning the game.

And sure enough the entire Shark family had joined in. Mommy and Daddy Shark boogied. Grandma and Grandpa Shark bopped. It was officially a Shark dance party!

"I had such a magical day," Baby Shark said. "But I think I'm ready to go home."

The Shark Family started to head home, but Mommy Shark had one last surprise. "Let's watch the sunset," she said.

As they poked their heads out of the water, they saw a giant rainbow. What a great surprise!

Grandpa Shark's Pirate Crew

One gloomy afternoon, Baby Shark didn't quite know what to do with himself. He had played with all his toys, eaten his entire lunch, and colored every piece of paper in his room. So he swam outside to look for something to do. That's when he noticed a treasure chest. "What's this doing here?" Baby Shark said.

Just then Baby Shark saw something move behind the treasure chest.

"Was that an eye patch?" Baby Shark said. "I better go check it out."

And when Baby Shark swam behind the treasure chest, he found . . .

"Grandpa Shark!?" Baby Shark squeaked. "Why are you wearing a pirate costume?"

"Ahoy, Baby Shark!" said Grandpa Shark. "I'm the Pirate Captain! Do yee dare hunt down me lost pirate crew?"

Baby Shark's eyes sparkled. "Oooh, a hide-and-hunt pirate game! You always have the best ideas, Grandpa Shark! I love hunting."

"Argh!" Grandpa Shark said. "Then this will be easy for yee, matey."

"I'm on it, Grandpa Shark," Baby Shark said as he swam off toward the horizon. "I'll definitely find your pirate crew. I mean, argh, I'll find yee pirate crew, ya scallywag!"

Baby Shark splashed toward a creepy cave at the bottom of the sea.

"Could someone be inside?" Baby Shark said. He was starting to feel a little nervous. It was such a gloomy day, and this cave was starting to look pretty spooky.

"Hello?" he called out. "Is anyone there?"

BRRRRAP! BRRRRRAP!

Baby Shark knew that sound from anywhere. "Daddy Shark? What are you doing here in this cave? You're not a pirate!"

Daddy Shark laughed. "Of course I'm not a pirate. I'm a trumpet player! This cave has great acoustics. Just listen to this!"

BRRRRAP!

Next Baby Shark swam past a forest of kelp and seaweed. And out of the corner of his eye, Baby Shark thought he saw a pirate hook!

"Could it be the pirate captain's crew?" he said. "Time to put my hunting skills to the test and find out."

"Grandma Shark!" Baby Shark said. "What are you doing here in this seaweed forest?"

Grandma Shark chuckled. "Hello, my precious Baby Shark! Well, I'm tending to my seaweed garden. It's high time I got rid of these pesky coral weeds."

"I guess you're not a pirate either," Baby Shark said.

"Nope!" she replied. "I'm just married to one."

Baby Shark continued on and found pretty seashells near the ocean floor. He noticed a tail zipping around the shells and behind the rocks.

"Oh, look!" he said. "This pirate must be collecting shells to decorate their pirate ship."

"I'm not letting this pirate get away," Baby Shark said. He cut through the water and bounced into an unsuspecting . . .

"Mommy Shark!" he said.

"Whoa! Be careful, Baby Shark," Mommy Shark said. "I don't want to get paint on you. I'm working on painting these seashells for our fishy neighbors."

Baby Shark sighed. "Where could Grandpa Shark's pirate crew be?"

Baby Shark was out of ideas. He didn't know where the
pirate crew was.

"Maybe I'm not such a good hunter after all," Baby Shark
said sadly.

He slowly paddled through a rocky part of the ocean when
he saw a giant sunken . . .

"Pirate ship!" he said.

"ARGH! You found us!" the pirate crew cheered. They had been hiding on the ship the entire time.

"And here comes our Capt'n," said Baby Crab. "Grandpa Shark!"

"Argh! Nice work, Baby Shark!" said Grandpa Shark. "You found me lost pirate crew. You're too good at hide-and-hunt!"

"I love hunting," Baby Shark said. "But I think I'd like to try and hide."

"Okay," Grandpa Shark said, "avast, yee scallywags, batten down the hatches! We are going on a shark hunt."

Later that afternoon, Grandpa Shark and his pirate crew looked and looked. But Baby Shark was nowhere to be found!

Even Mommy Shark, Daddy Shark, and Grandma Shark joined in the hunt for Baby Shark.

Where could he be hiding?

"YO-HO-HO!" Baby Shark cried as he appeared from out
of the rocks. "I am the official hide-and-hunt winner."

Grandpa Shark smiled. "And now the new Pirate Captain."

Everyone cheered as Grandpa Shark handed over his
captain's hat to Baby Shark.

"Thank you for an amazing day, Grandpa Shark," Baby Shark said. "You're the best grandpa ever."

"Of course, Capt'n," Grandpa Shark said. "Now what adventure should we go on next?"

Little Red Riding Shark

BUS

One bright morning, Baby Shark decided to visit Grandma Shark. So Mommy Shark gave him a basket of goodies to give her. She also put Baby Shark's favorite red hood on him. Then she swam Baby Shark to the bus stop.

Swishing goodbye with his tail, he swam onto the bus and was quickly on his way!

Baby Shark could hardly sit still. He had been wanting to visit Grandma Shark for a while, and now the day was finally here! He had never gone by himself before, and he was a little nervous.

"I'm a very brave shark," Baby Shark said to himself, "but I just hope I don't see a whale. They are so big, and I'm just a little shark. If I keep to my route, then I will be at Grandma's in no time."

As the bus moved along down the road, Baby Shark spotted some playful crabs.

"Hi!" Baby Shark said. "I'm on my way to visit Grandma Shark."

"How fun!" Daddy Crab said. "Tell Grandma Shark we said hello!"

"I love visiting Grandma Crab," Baby Crab said. "We color all day. I can hold all the crayons with one claw."

Baby Shark laughed as the bus continued on.

Next the bus drove past an adorable green turtle.

"Hello there," Baby Shark said. "I'm on my way to visit Grandma Shark."

"Grandma Turtle is my best friend," she told him. "We love to bake her famous snap turtle cookies!"

Baby Shark smiled. He loved hearing everyone's stories about how much they loved their grandmas.

Soon the bus headed into a tunnel. Baby Shark knew that meant they were almost to Grandma's house! But the tunnel was pretty dark and spooky.

"This is my least favorite part of the trip," Baby Shark said.

There was only a little bit of ocean left to travel.
But Baby Shark started to get a little nervous again.

"What if the bus gets lost?" Baby Shark said. "What
if I never make it to Grandma Shark's house? Or worst
of all . . . what if I see a whale?!"

Baby Shark got so worried that he began to cry.

Just then Baby Shark saw a faint glow in the dark tunnel. The glow got brighter and brighter. It was a group of electric eels!

"What's wrong, Baby Shark?" they asked him.

"I'm scared," he said.

"Don't be scared, Baby Shark," they told him.

"Look, you're finally at the end of the tunnel!"
PHEW! The bus had finally made its way out of
the tunnel.

Baby Shark wasn't feeling quite so scared anymore.
In fact, he was starting to get excited about seeing Grandma
Shark again.

"Maybe you'll go on a treasure hunt with your grandma
and learn about ocean animals you haven't even met yet,"
Mommy Eel said.

"Or maybe you'll do puzzles," Daddy Eel said.

"I can't wait to do all of those things. See you later, Eel family!" Baby Shark said, waving goodbye to his new friends. "Man, that tunnel was scary. I'm glad I'm feeling better now."

Baby Shark put his fins on his hips. "I'm a brave shark. A dark tunnel can't scare me. Or even a whale!"

"AAAAHHHHHHH!" Baby Shark screamed as he saw a giant whale behind him.

"AAAAHHHHHHH!" Mommy Whale screamed. "You scared me, Baby Shark!"

"S-s-scared you?" Baby Shark said, shaking. "You scared me! I'm just trying to get to my grandma's house."

"Yes, I've been trying to catch you all day," Mommy Whale said. "I wanted to give you these flowers to give to Grandma Shark. She gave me flowers from her garden the other day, and I thought I would return the favor."

Baby Shark smiled. He had been so silly to be scared of such a nice whale. The two friends talked until the bus came to a stop right in front of Grandma Shark's house.

"Well, this is your stop," Mommy Whale said. "When you give Grandma Shark those flowers, tell her I said hello!"

"I will," said Baby Shark, waving goodbye.

"I can't wait to see my Grandma Shark—finally!"

"That reminds me," Mommy Whale said. "I need to pay Grandma Whale a visit soon. I used to love when she read me stories. She did all the funny voices!"

"Mine does, too!" Baby Shark replied. He swished his tail as he made his way toward Grandma Shark's house.

"There you are, Baby Shark!" said Grandma Shark when she saw him. Baby Shark was talking a mile a minute.

"I can't wait to color, bake cookies, go on a treasure hunt," Baby Shark said, "or maybe we could even do a puzzle?!"

"How about we read a story?" Grandma Shark suggested. "I know a good one about a big whale!"

pinkfong
BABY SHARK™
Shark Family
Bakery

A tasty oven-baked smell filled the ocean from the Shark Family Bakery truck. Grandpa Shark's cupcakes were the talk of the sea, and he had just baked a fresh batch.

"Get your freshly baked cupcakes!" Grandpa Shark shouted.

Grandpa Shark was a very busy baker. He did everything himself. From measuring the sugar to picking out flavor, each cupcake had Grandpa Shark's special touch.

DING! The timer went off. Grandpa Shark smiled as he pulled the tray out of the oven. "Another piping hot batch of delicious cupcakes," he said.

"Ahem, I was first in line," a pushy seahorse said.

"Yeah, and I'm second!" a sweet orange fish said.

"My favorite time of day is cupcake time."

The smell of Grandpa Shark's cupcakes drew a huge crowd. Animals from across the ocean gathered around Grandpa Shark's bakery truck! Sure enough, Grandpa Shark quickly sold out of his famous cupcakes.

"We need more cupcakes. Come back later this afternoon," Grandpa Shark told everyone. "I promise that everyone here will get a cupcake."

"Hi, Grandpa Shark!" Baby Shark called as he swam up to the truck. "Do you think I could get one of your famous cupcakes?"

"Baby Shark!" Grandpa Shark said, relieved. "Would you be able to help me make more cupcakes?"

Baby Shark couldn't wait to get started. He loved to bake, but he loved helping Grandpa Shark even more. Grandpa Shark walked him through the recipe for the batter.

"One spoon of sugar, two spoons of mud, and three spoons of water bubbles!" Grandpa Shark said.

Grandpa Shark put the cupcakes in the oven. Baby Shark watched as the tiny cakes began to quickly rise.

DING! The timer went off.

"And just like that, tasty hot cupcakes are ready!" Grandpa Shark said.

"Good thing we got these cupcakes made just in time," Baby Shark said. "That was the last of the ingredients."

The smell of cupcakes spread across the ocean. Everyone headed back to the Shark Family Bakery truck for their cupcake.

Oh no! The pushy seahorse brought the entire seahorse family!

Grandpa Shark handed out the fresh batch of cupcakes and didn't realize that there weren't going to be enough cupcakes for everyone.

"Great Neptune!" he said. "We are one cupcake short. This sweet little orange fish waited for his cupcake all day."

The sweet orange fish began to cry. "I was going to give the cupcake to my baby brother," he said. "Now my surprise is totally ruined."

The little fish's story gave Grandpa Shark a heavy heart.

"We need to get this sweet fish a cupcake, quick," Grandpa Shark said. "A little fish with a heart this big deserves a fresh cupcake. But we are all out of sugar, mud, and water bubbles."

Just then Baby Shark had a brilliant idea!

"What if we asked our customers to help us?" Baby Shark said. "Surely they know how sad it would be to miss out on your famous cupcakes. Right, Grandpa Shark?"

"Amazing idea, Baby Shark!" said Grandpa Shark.

"Listen up, everyone!" Grandpa Shark shouted from the bakery truck. "We need a pail of sparkly sugar, a pail of gooey mud, and a pail of bubbly water bubbles. This poor fish needs a cupcake to bring to his brother. I know he would do the same for any one of you."

The ocean animals nodded their heads. Everyone deserved to have a taste of Grandpa Shark's delicious cupcakes. Especially someone as kind as the little orange fish.

The animals quickly set to work collecting the ingredients. A striped blue fish found the mud, a yellow fish found the water bubbles, and . . .

The pushy seahorse found the sugar! "I'm so sorry," the seahorse said, "it's my fault that the sweet orange fish did not get his cupcake. I hope this can make it right."

Baby Shark quickly made the cupcake batter. Then Grandpa Shark put the cupcake in the oven. It quickly began to rise!

They did it! But Baby Shark was sad. "I wish we could've made two cupcakes," he said. "One for the fish's baby brother and the other for the fish."

Grandpa Shark just smiled. "Come look, Baby Shark."

When Baby Shark looked inside the oven, he couldn't believe what he saw!

It was a *giant* cupcake!

The sweet orange fish would have more than enough cupcake for his entire fish family to enjoy.

"Thank you for this amazing cupcake," the sweet orange fish said. "The Shark Family Bakery is truly the best bakery under the sea!"

Grandpa Shark smiled. "Come back soon!"

The Shark Tooth Fairy

"Good morning!" Baby Shark said as he swam out of bed. He stretched out his fins and let out a yawn. He had a big smile because he was excited to go outside and play with his friends. But when he smiled, Baby Shark felt like something was different . . .

Baby Shark's tooth was gone!

"Wha-what happened to my too-f?" Baby Shark cried.

"Did someone take it? I need to get it back!"

Baby Shark did not like to lose things. Just then a school of fish swam by.

"What happened, Baby Shark?" they asked.

Baby Shark was sad. "I lost my too-f. I fell asleep with my too-f last night, and when I woke up, my too-f was gone!"

"How strange," said the fish. "You should probably go look for it."

So Baby Shark set off to look for his lost tooth.

"Where could it be?" Baby Shark wondered. "Maybe I lost it yesterday when I was building my sandcastle."

Baby Shark swam toward the sandcastle. He swam through it, over it, and around it! But the tooth was not there.

"Maybe I lost it when I was playing in the rock garden," said Baby Shark.

So he swam toward the rock garden. There were so many rocks that the tooth could be under any one of them! Baby Shark looked under almost every rock. But the tooth was not there.

Baby Shark couldn't find his tooth anywhere! After searching all morning, Baby Shark began to get really worried. He was going to have to find Mommy Shark and tell her what happened.

"What will Mommy Shark say!" cried Baby Shark. "She doesn't like when I lose things. And my tee-f are very important for a healthy shark."

"Will Mommy Shark be mad?" Baby Shark wondered. "Or will she be scared?"

Either way, Baby Shark did not want to get in trouble. So he decided to keep his lost tooth a secret.

That night, Baby Shark swam into bed. He had managed to hide his smile from Mommy Shark and Daddy Shark all day.

But when Baby Shark fell asleep, he had a bad dream. He dreamed he lost all his teeth—he was toothless like Grandma Shark!

"Ahhhhhhh!" Baby Shark cried.
Suddenly he woke up from his bad dream.

"That's it," Baby Shark said, "I need to tell Mommy Shark what happened. I shouldn't be keeping secrets from her. She loves me and will help me even if I do get in trouble."

So Baby Shark swam out of bed and found Mommy Shark. "Mommy, my too-f is gone!" he said.

Mommy Shark did something that Baby Shark was not expecting. Mommy Shark smiled! Then she hugged Baby Shark.

"It's okay, Baby Shark," Mommy Shark said.

"You don't need to get so upset. Maybe it fell out in the middle of the night. We should find it and put it under your pillow for the shark tooth fairy."

"The shark too-f fairy?" Baby Shark asked. "What's a shark too-f fairy?"

Mommy Shark smiled. "The shark tooth fairy is a magical ocean creature. She looks like a fish and has blue fins. She carries around a magic wand with a shark tooth on the tip of it. Her job is to take your baby teeth and replace them with a coin under your pillow."

"My too-f must have fallen out when I was sleeping," said Baby Shark. "I haven't looked next to my bed yet!"

Baby Shark quickly swam toward his bed. There it was! Baby Shark found his tooth!

"It had fallen on the floor!" Baby Shark said.

That night, Baby Shark got ready for bed.
"I'm going to put the tooth under my pillow
just like Mommy Shark told me," said Baby Shark.
He carefully placed the shark tooth under his pillow.
He snuggled under the blankets and quickly fell
asleep. Good night, Baby Shark!

That night, while Baby Shark slept, the shark tooth fairy crept toward his bed.

With a *SWOOSH* of her magic wand, Baby Shark's tooth appeared in her fin. She *SWOOSHED* her magic wand again. The wand began to glow brighter and brighter. Then just as suddenly as she had appeared, the shark tooth fairy was gone!

When Baby Shark woke up, he quickly checked under his pillow, and . . .

. . . there was a shiny gold coin! "Mommy Shark was right!" Baby Shark said. "The shark too-f fairy did visit me last night. My too-f is gone, and she left me a gold coin. I've got to show Mommy Shark!"

Baby Shark swam as fast as he could until he bounced right into Mommy Shark.

"Mommy! Mommy!" Baby Shark cried. "The shark too-f fairy left me a gold coin, look! Maybe I could buy myself a new too-f."

Mommy Shark giggled. "Oh, Baby Shark, don't worry. In time, you will grow a new tooth."

Thank you, shark tooth fairy!

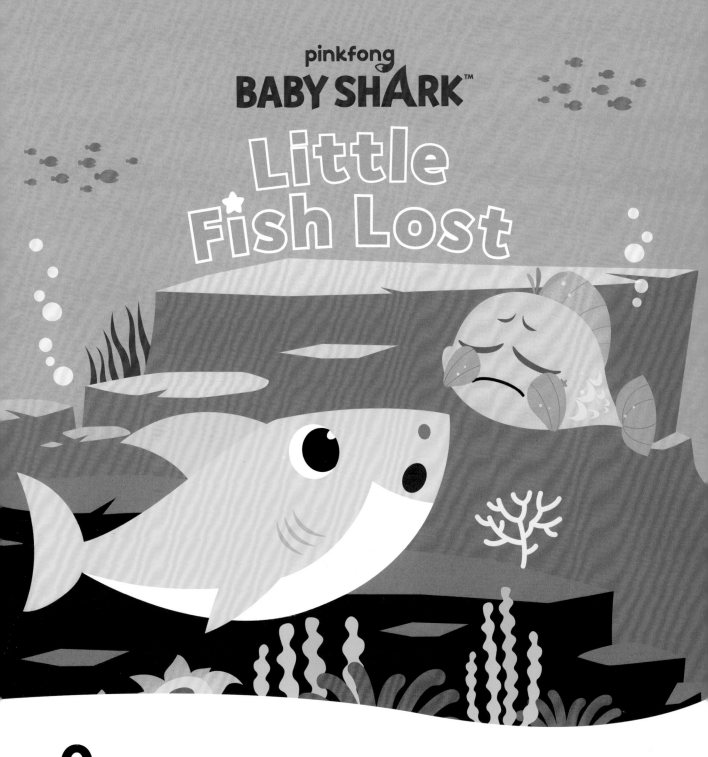

pinkfong
BABY SHARK™
Little Fish Lost

One day, Baby Shark was swimming home from school when he came upon a little yellow fish. When Baby Shark got closer, he noticed that he was crying.

"Boo-hoo!" the little fish cried.

"Oh no!" said Baby Shark. "What's wrong, little fish? Why are you crying?"

The fish wiped a tear away. "I'm lost."

"How did you get lost?" Baby Shark asked.

"A wave swept me away from home," the fish replied. "I live in a big reef. Mommy Fish will be so worried."

"It's okay," Baby Shark said. "It's easy to find a big reef. We can see it from the sky."

The little fish sniffled. He was confused. "How am I going to get up to the sky?"

Baby Shark grabbed the fish's fin. "Come with me!"

Baby Shark took the lost fish to the playground and swam him over to the seesaw.

"A seesaw goes high!" Baby Shark said.

The fish smiled. "You're right. A seesaw could help us get to the sky!"

As the seesaw went up and down, the little fish flew up and flapped his fins. He tried to get as high as he could, but he didn't reach the sky.

"What are we going to do?" the little fish said sadly.
"Don't worry," Baby Shark said. "Hmmm, let me think . . ."

"I've got it!" Baby Shark cried. "We need a ladder to the sky!"

"Huh?" the little fish said.

"Follow me!" said Baby Shark, swimming off. The little fish followed him all the way to Daddy Octopus.

"Hello, friends!" said Daddy Octopus. "Would you like an ice cream cone? I've got every flavor under the sea."

"Thanks, but maybe later," said Baby Shark. "Can you help my friend? He needs to reach the sky, and you have the longest arms of anyone I know!"

"That's so sweet that you thought of me," said Daddy Octopus. "Here, do me a favor, hold these ice cream cones."

Daddy Octopus handed the ice creams to Baby Shark and
the little fish, and then he stretched two of his eight tentacles
up as high as he could. They only reached the top of his head.

"It looks like my arms are too short to reach the sky,"
said Daddy Octopus. "But maybe Mommy Whale can help!"

"Oh, hello, Baby Shark," Mommy Whale said as Baby Shark and the little fish swam up to her. "And who is this?"

"This is my new friend," said Baby Shark. "Do you think you could help him? He needs to reach the sky so he can find his way home."

"Of course," said Mommy Whale. "Hop on my back!"

"Hold tight! Here we go!" Mommy Whale said as she zoomed to the surface of the water.

Then with a big *WHOOSH*, she sprayed water into the air through her blowhole. Baby Shark and the little fish soared up high!

"We're flying!" cried Baby Shark. "I can see the entire ocean from up here!"

The two friends had finally reached the sky! The little fish squinted as he looked out over the water, then suddenly . . .

"There!" the fish shouted. "I see the reef!"

Then just as quickly as they rose into the air, Baby Shark and the little fish fell back into the water with a big *SPLASH!*

"Follow me, Baby Shark!" the fish said. "The reef is this way!"

"Mommy Fish!" the little fish cried as he hugged his Mommy at the coral reef.

"Thank you, Baby Shark," said Mommy Fish. "I was so worried."

"I'm glad he's home," Baby Shark said. "It's getting late. I better go before my Mommy Shark gets worried."

The little fish smiled. "I'm so happy
to have a friend like you, Baby Shark."
"Goodbye, Baby Shark!"

"Mommy Shark loves to cuddle, and Daddy Shark loves to play," Baby Shark said. "Grandma Shark sings, and Grandpa Shark bakes. Everyone is so unique and so special to me for all different reasons. This is going to be a lot of work, but it will be totally worth it to see the look on their faces!"

With that, Baby Shark set to work.

Baby Shark made a card for Mommy Shark first. He loved Mommy Shark because she gave the best hugs and kisses.

"I know exactly how to decorate Mommy Shark's card," Baby Shark said. "First I'll draw a big heart because I love her so much. Next I'll add pink glitter to the heart so that the card matches her. And finally I'll draw a picture of Mommy Shark smiling. She always makes me smile."

I LOVE YOU

Mommy

Next Baby Shark made a card for Daddy Shark. He loved Daddy Shark because he was fun to play with. Baby Shark and Daddy Shark's games of tag were legendary. If it were up to Baby Shark, he would spend all day chasing Daddy Shark through the deep blue sea.

Lastly he made a card for his best friend, William. Baby Shark loved William because he was one funny fish!

"On happy days and sad days, William always finds a way to make me smile," Baby Shark said. "So I'm going to draw my favorite memory of William. It was when he showed up to my birthday party wearing a silly hula skirt!"

I LOVE YOU

William

Baby Shark stretched out his fins and yawned a big yawn. He was getting tired from making all these beautiful cards. The sun had started to set, and it was time to go to bed. Baby Shark looked down at all the beautiful cards he made.

"I guess I'll have to give these to everyone tomorrow," he said. "I won't be able to sleep! I'm too excited to see their reactions."

But when Baby Shark put on his pajamas and climbed into bed, he could hardly keep his eyes open. So he softly closed them and drifted off to sleep.

The next morning, Baby Shark
swam right out of bed.
"Good morning, ocean!" he said.
"Today is the day. I can't wait to
give everyone their cards!"

So Baby Shark grabbed all the cards and swam out the front door. He needed to find everyone.

"Mommy Shark! Daddy Shark!" he called out. "Where are you guys?"

When he finally found his friends and family, Baby Shark couldn't believe his eyes . . .

Mommy, Daddy, Grandma, Grandpa, Baby Turtle, and William had made a giant card for Baby Shark, too!

"We love you, Baby Shark!" they said.

"We worked together to make you this card," said Mommy Shark. "We had no idea that you were making us cards, too!"

Baby Shark's heart was so full. "Thank you, everyone. I love you so much!"

Grandma Shark's Magic Wand

POOF!

Grandma Shark was having a great day. That morning, she had decided to dress up in her witch's hat and cape. And when she was digging her hat out of the attic, she came across her old magic wand.

"With just a small flick and a *WHOOSH*, my magic wand is in working order again," Grandma Shark said. "My wand can do anything!"

As she swam through the water, Grandma Shark came across a little baby fish.

"Are you okay?" Grandma Shark asked. "A baby fish shouldn't be out here all alone."

"I was swimming with my mommy," cried the baby fish. "But I lost her."

"Hush, hush," Grandma Shark said. "Don't worry, dear, I'll help you find her."

The baby fish wiped his tears away. "Really? How?"

"With my magic wand, of course!" Grandma Shark said. She swished her tail, waved her wand, and the star of her wand began to glow. Then suddenly . . .

"There you are!" the mommy fish said as she swam up to her baby. "I've been looking for you everywhere."

The baby fish couldn't believe it. "Wow! Thanks, Grandma Shark!"

Grandma Shark was happy to help her fellow ocean animals. As she continued her swim through the water, she came across a pink fish.

"Hello there!" Grandma Shark called out. "How are you today?"

"Not so good," the pink fish said. "I think my house blew away. When I left my house this morning, I had a house. But when I came back this afternoon, my house was gone!"

"Oh dear!" said Grandma Shark. "That's quite a shock. Here, let me help you."

"But how?" the pink fish asked. "Do you know how to build houses?"

Grandma Shark giggled. "No, silly, I'll just use my magic wand."

POOF! And just like that, the pink fish had a brand-new house.

"Thank you so much!" said the pink fish. "This is such a fabulous house. You must come over sometime, and I'll show you how I'm going to decorate it."

It made Grandma Shark so happy that her magic could help all these ocean friends. She was so happy, she started to dance. Then she twirled her wand. But oh no . . .

Her wand fell down, down, down! All the way to the ocean floor. When it hit the sandy bottom, it *SNAPPED* right in half.

"Oh dear!" said Grandma Shark. "My magic wand is broken. Maybe if I find some tape, I can fix it."

Wouldn't you know it, Grandma Shark found tape and wrapped it around her broken wand. *POOF!* Just like that, Grandma Shark fixed her broken wand.

"That should do it," said Grandma Shark. "I hope this doesn't affect the magic . . . oh, hello, Baby Shark!"

At that moment, Baby Shark spotted his grandma and quickly swam over to talk to her.

"You found your old magic wand!" Baby Shark said. "Hey, can you turn my ball into a friend? That would be so cool!"

"Hmm," Grandma Shark said. "I hope this works . . ."

WHOOSH!
SQUEAK!
POOF!
"Oh no!" Grandma Shark cried.
"My broken wand turned Baby Shark
into a toy! Don't worry,
Baby Shark, I'll fix this!"

Grandma Shark concentrated as hard as she could. "Wish, wish! Light, light! Baby Shark, ahoy! Magic wand, make it right. Make this toy a boy!"

As Grandma Shark said her magic spell, the wand began to sparkle and glow. It was working.

POOF!

"Phew!" Grandma Shark said. "You are back to normal, Baby Shark."

"Back to what?" Baby Shark asked. He had no idea that he had turned into a toy. And maybe that was okay.

"Come on, Grandma Shark!" Baby Shark said. "Can you use your magic wand to help me build my sandcastle?"

Grandma Shark was worried that her magic wand might mess up again. But she couldn't resist that adorable Baby Shark face. She would do anything for him!

"Of course, dear," she said.

"Now," Grandma Shark said.
"Let's see if it will work this time!"
WHOOSH!
SQUEAK!
POOF!
"Oh no," Grandma Shark said.
"That didn't sound good."

"Ahhhhhh!" Baby Shark cried. "My sandcastle is shrinking!"

Instead of making the sandcastle bigger, Grandma Shark's broken magic wand had made it smaller.

"This wand just needs a little bit of help," Grandma Shark said, smiling. "I know what to do. Will you help me, Baby Shark?"

Baby Shark smiled. "Anything for you, Grandma Shark!"

"Good," Grandma Shark said. "Now repeat after me, Baby Shark. Swish, swish! Glow, glow! Baby Shark, sing! Magic wand, let it flow. Make a castle for a king!"

Grandma Shark and Baby Shark chanted the spell together. And suddenly the sandcastle began to grow bigger!

Baby Shark giggled. "Thanks for a magical day, Grandma Shark!"

Police Sharks

One bright morning, Daddy Shark had a big surprise for Baby Shark.

"My own police hat?!" Baby Shark cried. "I've always wanted one of these."

"And I got one for myself, too," said Daddy Shark. "How about we go on patrol today. Maybe we could find some ocean friends that need our help."

With that, Baby Shark and Daddy Shark set off to patrol the ocean.

WEEE OOH! WEEE OOH!

Suddenly a wailing siren went off. Someone was in trouble!

"Police Sharks on duty!" Baby Shark said. "We keep the peace in the ocean!"

The Police Sharks took off with their tails swishing through the water.

"Don't worry citizens," said Daddy Shark. "The police sharks are on their way!"

Peeking out from some coral, a fish family were frantically flapping their fins.

"Police Sharks! Thank Neptune you're here! The Octopus Sisters are fighting!" said one of the fish.

"The Octopus sisters?" Baby Shark said. "That doesn't sound like them."

But then Police Sharks heard the cries for help. They were on the case!

"There's nothing to fear, the Police Sharks are on the way!"
Baby Shark said, swimming even faster.

"Whoa!" Daddy Shark said, giggling. "Wait for me, Baby
Shark!"

It made Daddy Shark happy to see Baby Shark having so
much fun.

When the Police Sharks arrived on the scene, they couldn't believe their eyes. The Octopus Sisters were entangled in a tentacle fight!

"Sisters, sisters!" Daddy Shark said, trying to break up the fight. "We do not fight in the ocean!"

"We aren't fighting," explained one of the Octopus Sisters. "We just got tangled up in the dark down here."

"I knew it," Baby Shark told Daddy Shark. "The Octopus Sisters love each other. They would never fight!"

"You were right, Baby Shark," Daddy Shark said. "Now let's get these sisters untangled."

The Police Sharks set right to work. Daddy Shark
untangled one sister's arms, and Baby Shark untangled the
other sister's arms. Slowly but surely, the Octopus sisters
began to free each one of their eight tentacles.

" . . . five, six, seven, eight!" Baby Shark counted. "There
you go. All eight tentacles are free. Well, actually, I guess it
would be sixteen tentacles."

"Oh, thank you, Police Sharks!" said the Octopus Sisters. "We thought we were going to be stuck like that forever!"

"No need to thank us," Daddy Shark said. "We were just doing our duty."

The Octopus Sisters smiled and giggled as the Police Sharks set off to help more ocean friends.

"This is so much fun!" said Baby Shark.

"I'm so glad," said Daddy Shark. "Not only are we having fun, but we are also helping ocean animals at the same time. I'm so proud of you, Baby Shark. High-fin me!"

Baby Shark beamed as he high-finned his dad. "You make patrolling the oceans fun, Daddy Shark. Come on, our mission isn't over yet."

WEEE OOH! WEEE OOH!

The sirens blared again. Someone else was in trouble!

"We're on our way," said Daddy Shark. "No ocean is too deep!"

The Police Sharks swam as quickly as they could to the scene of the crime. The Hammerhead Shark's house was an old sunken ship at the bottom of the sea. When they arrived, the Police Sharks heard a big commotion coming from the front of the ship.

"Look! I see a tail. Someone is trying to break into the house through this tiny hole!" Daddy Shark said. Then Daddy Shark began to shout. "Put your fins up! You're surrounded by Police Sharks!"

"Hmm," Baby Shark said. "Something seems fishy here."

The thief didn't listen to Daddy Shark. They kept thrashing wildly in the tiny hole, tossing poor Hammerhead Shark's things around inside.

"Okay, Baby Shark, you take one side of the tail, and I'll grab the other," said Daddy Shark. "Now on the count of three, pull as hard as you can."

Baby Shark nodded and quickly grabbed the thief's tail. "One, two, three!"

The Police Sharks successfully pulled out the intruder only to discover it wasn't a thief at all. It was . . .

"Hammerhead Shark!" Daddy Shark said. "Why were you breaking into your own house?"

"Thank you for freeing me," said the grateful Hammerhead. "I fell through this hole and got stuck!"

Another ocean friend saved! And just like that, Daddy Shark and Baby Shark swam to find their next case.

Later that afternoon, the Police Sharks heard the siren wail again. But when they arrived on the scene, no one was in trouble. Instead, it was the Octopus Sisters and the Hammerhead Shark waiting for them. The ocean friends were throwing the Police Sharks their very own awards ceremony.

"Put your hands together for the best Police Sharks!" said the Octopus Sisters.

"And for your bravery, we are awarding you your very own Police Shark badges," said the Hammerhead Shark.

"Thank you, citizens," said Daddy Shark. "But this award should really go to Baby Shark. His instincts when it comes to solving cases makes him a truly special Police Shark."

Baby Shark smiled as Daddy Shark placed the official Police Shark badge on his chest.

Baby Shark looked down at his new badge with pride. "The real reward was having a fun day with my Daddy Shark."

Family Orchestra

It was a very chatty day in the ocean. A group of fish could not stop talking about the most exciting event of the season.

"The family orchestra concert is tonight!" said a purple fish.

"Oh, how fin-tastic!" said another fish. "I wonder if Baby Shark will perform this year. He is amazing!"

WHOOSH!

Just then Baby Shark swam by the group of fish. Tonight was his first time performing in the family orchestra concert! He had his bow tie on and was looking good.

"Come and see the Shark Family Orchestra!" he called out to the fishy fans. "It's going to be magical!"

"Wait for us, Baby Shark!" called out Mommy Shark.
Daddy Shark swam alongside her. "Come on, you two,
we don't want to be late."

It was time to take the stage. Baby Shark was the first musician to tune his instrument. He was playing the marimba. Baby Shark tapped the wooden keys with two mallets.

PLINK! PLINK! PLINK!

"I'm ready," said Baby Shark.

"Mommy Shark here on the clarinet," Mommy Shark said. "Listen to my notes flow!"

TU, TU, TU!

"Don't forget about the flute," Daddy Shark said. "Check this out."

TOOTLE-TOO! TOOTLE-TOO!

"Don't forget about us," said Grandma Shark as she took the stage with Grandpa Shark. Grandma Shark played a lot of instruments, but tonight she was playing the trumpet.

"It's Baby Shark's first orchestra performance, so I'm going to make it special," said Grandpa Shark. He grabbed the double bass and began to pull the bow over the long strings.

"Ahem!" said a booming voice behind them. "And no one can forget about me! I'm the singer."

Of course," Baby Shark said. "You're the prima donna! The lead singer. "

The prima donna smiled. "Thank you for that fabulous introduction, Baby Shark. Now, places everyone. The concert is about to begin."

The entire orchestra was tuned and ready to go. The giant curtain lifted, and the Shark Family Orchestra was revealed to the audience!

The players looked to their conductor. His job was to direct the entire performance.

Let the concert begin!

The Shark Family Orchestra began to play the first song. Everything was going great. Baby Shark was hitting the right notes, Daddy Shark was carrying the melody, and Grandpa Shark was keeping the bass line.

But then the prima donna began to sing.

"La, la, la, laaaa-eck!"

Cough! Cough!

"Oh no!" said Baby Shark. "The prima donna has lost her voice."

Shocked, the Shark Family Orchestra stopped playing. The audience began to mumble and grumble. What was going on?

Grandpa Shark began to whisper to Baby Shark. "What are we going to do?"

The conductor was speechless, too.

"In all my years of conducting, this has never happened before!" he said to himself. But he straightened his bow tie and turned to the audience. "Ladies and gentlemen, please remain seated while we work out this—um—tiny, little problem."

The family orchestra concert was turning into a disaster.
But Baby Shark had an idea.

"Let's try a different song," he whispered to himself.
"This one will surely get the prima donna's voice back."

He began to play his marimba softly and sang along.
"Baby Shark, doo-doo-doo-doo-doo-doo . . ."

Mommy Shark smiled. She started to play her clarinet.
TU, TU, TU!

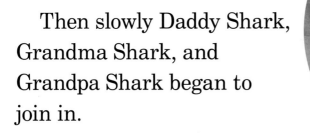

Then slowly Daddy Shark, Grandma Shark, and Grandpa Shark began to join in.

They played their instruments and sang along with Baby Shark.
"Baby Shark, doo-doo-doo-doo-doo-doo . . ."

Baby Shark looked back at the prima donna. She looked very nervous.

"You can do it," he whispered. "You've got this. You know the song. Just sing with your whole heart, and the music will flow through you."

The prima donna looked at Baby Shark and then looked back at the waiting audience and frightened conductor. She cleared her throat and tried to sing again.

"B-Ba-Baby Shark, doo-doo-doo-doo-doo-doo!"

She did it—the prima donna's voice was back!

The orchestra played the entire song, and when it was over, the conductor turned to the audience, triumphant. "Ladies and gentlemen, let's hear it for the Shark Family Orchestra!"

The audience erupted in cheers. The prima donna took a big sweeping bow and then pointed her fin toward Baby Shark. "And most important, let's hear it for our newest addition to the orchestra—Baby Shark!"

pinkfong
BABY SHARK™
Balloons and Friends

It was a beautiful morning, and Baby Shark was ready to play outside! So he left his house to look for his friends.

"They usually hang out by the sandcastle," Baby Shark said to himself. But when he swam over to the sandcastle, they were nowhere to be found.

Where could they be?

Baby Shark looked and looked. He was beginning to get very bored.

"I am so bored!" he said. "I have no friends to play with."

Frustrated, Baby Shark sank to the sea floor and buried his face in the soft sand. But suddenly he saw something out of the corner of his eye.

"A treasure chest?!" Baby Shark cried. "Now this is exciting."

Just then the treasure chest began to rumble when *CREAK!* It opened up. Baby Shark watched in awe as four balloons floated out of the treasure chest!

"Wow!" Baby Shark said. "Colorful balloons!"

Baby Shark quickly grabbed the balloons. He decided to tie the balloons to his tail so they wouldn't float away. He swam as fast as he could, and the balloons trailed behind him.

"Wheeee!" he said. "These balloons are so fun."

"Help!" shouted a voice in the distance.

Baby Shark stopped swimming and looked up to see where the cry for help was coming from.

"Gosh!" Baby Shark said. "I've got to help whoever is in trouble."

When Baby Shark followed the voice, he came upon a large coral hill. But wait, who is that on top of the coral hill?

"Baby Turtle?!" Baby Shark said, recognizing his friend. "She's going too fast!" Baby Shark watched as his friend slid down the hill and landed with a *THUD* at the bottom.

Baby Shark rushed over to help his friend. "Are you okay, Baby Turtle?"

"Ouch!" Baby Turtle said as her eyes started to well up with tears. "I-I-I hit my head."

"Here, let me help you," said Baby Shark. He put a bandage on Baby Turtle's boo-boo. Then he gave her a yellow balloon.

"I feel much better now," said Baby Turtle. "Thank you for helping me, Baby Shark! And thank you for my beautiful yellow balloon."

"Hooray!" Baby Shark said.

Baby Shark and Baby Turtle giggled together.

Just then the two friends heard someone else cry out for help. They swam over to see a squid playing a mean joke on Baby Shark's friend, Baby Seahorse!

"Don't worry, Baby Seahorse," Baby Shark said.
"We are here to help! Shoo you silly old octopus! Shoo!"

The squid swam away in a huff. The two ocean friends went to see if Baby Seahorse was alright. "You poor thing," said Baby Turtle. Baby Seahorse was covered head to tail in squid ink.

The friends helped wash the ink off Baby Seahorse. All squeaky clean!

To make Baby Seahorse feel better, Baby Shark gave him a red balloon.

"Wow, thank you," Baby Seahorse said. "I feel much better now. Watch me make bubbles as I swim with my red balloon!"

Baby Seahorse swam in a figure eight, blowing and popping bubbles as he went. The friends giggled together.

But then the ocean friends heard a voice crying in the distance. When they swam over, they spotted Baby Whale! He was all alone on the seesaw.

"No one will play with me!" Baby Whale cried on one side of the seesaw. "I'm so lonely. I wish I had friends to play with."

"Gosh!" Baby Shark said. "We will play with you, Baby Whale. Here, take my green balloon."

And with that, Baby Shark tied the green balloon around
Baby Whale. Then the ocean friends sat on the other side of
the seesaw. They began to move the seesaw up and down, up
and down.

"Wheeee!" Baby Whale shouted. "This is so much fun!
Look at how my balloon bounces."

"Thank you, Baby Shark," said Baby Whale. "You've completely turned my day around. I was so lonely, but now, look at all my new friends."

"Me too!" said Baby Turtle. "Baby Shark helped me when I fell down the coral hill."

Baby Seahorse smiled. "Baby Shark helped me, too, when a squid played a mean joke on me."

Baby Shark couldn't believe it. He was having so much fun with his new ocean friends. These colorful balloons were the key to bringing everyone together.

"Wow, these must be some magical friendship balloons," Baby Shark said, giggling. "They each helped an ocean friend in a special way."

For the rest of the day, the ocean friends played together. They danced to music, sang songs, and laughed at silly jokes.

The colorful balloons made playtime extra special because it reminded the ocean pals of Baby Shark's kindness and friendship.

"So much for being bored!" Baby Shark cheered.

Goodnight, Baby Shark

It had been a very long day. Baby Shark and his two best friends, Baby Turtle and William, were in an epic game of hide-and-seek.

"Okay, now try to find me!" Baby Shark said. Baby Turtle and William were exhausted.

"You're impossible to find," William said. "We will be looking all night!"

"Baby Shark!" Mommy Shark called out. "It's time to come home now."

"But we are still playing," Baby Shark said. He was not ready to go inside.

"You can play tomorrow. It's time to eat dinner," she said.

Baby Shark was sad to say goodbye to his friends. But he would see them again tomorrow. He quickly swam inside and got ready for dinner.

First he washed his hands and dried them.

Then he sat down at the dinner table and ate everything on his plate. Yum!

Next it was time for Baby Shark to brush his teeth. He had a special toothbrush that could get in between his sharp shark teeth.

"Look, Daddy Shark got me new toothpaste," Baby Shark said. "It's seaweed flavor—fin-tastic!"

And finally he got his pajamas on. He loved being cozy. One of his favorite things was his blue pillow. He couldn't sleep without it.

"I'm all ready for bed," Baby Shark said. "But I'm not tired at all."

"Shhhhh, shhhh, shhhh" Mommy Shark cooed as she tucked Baby Shark into bed. "Just count the bubbles. You'll fall asleep in no time."

She kissed Baby Shark on the cheek and patted his head.

Baby Shark tried to do what Mommy Shark said.

He counted the bubbles that floated above him.

One, two, three, four . . .

But Baby Shark kept losing count. And the bubbles kept getting all jumbled around in his head.

"Do you want Daddy Shark to come in, too?" asked Mommy Shark.

Mommy Shark called Daddy Shark over to Baby Shark's side. He swam over to Baby Shark and kissed him on the cheek and patted his head.

"How you doing, buddy?" Daddy Shark said sweetly.

"I'm not tired, Daddy," said Baby Shark matter-of-factly.

"Maybe it's too dark in here," Daddy Shark said. "What if I turn on your night-light?"

Daddy Shark swam over to a passing school of glow fish. He herded them next to Baby Shark's bed. The tiny fish gave off the perfect glow of soft light.

Baby Shark felt a little better as he snuggled his pillow, but he was still awake.

"Let me ask Grandma Shark," Daddy Shark said. "She will know what to do."

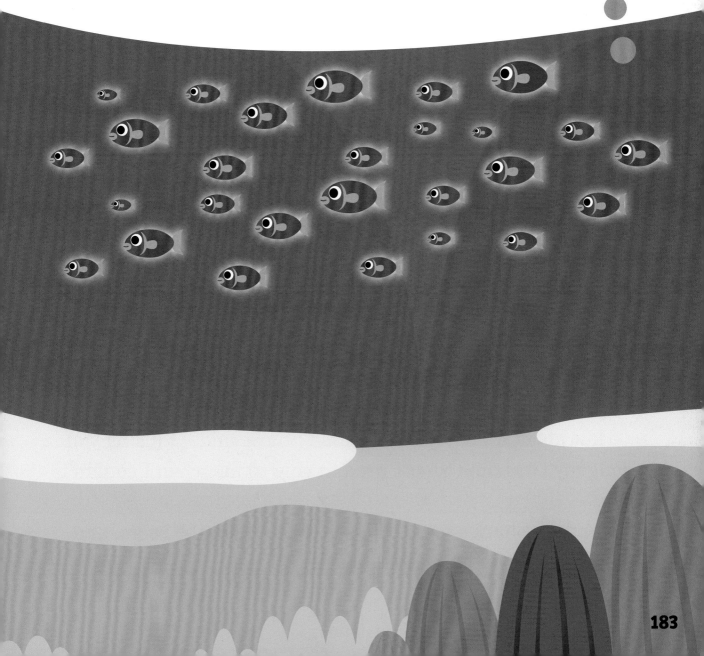

Daddy Shark asked Grandma Shark to help. She loved her grandson very much and was happy to help him.

"How about a lullaby?" Grandma Shark said. "I'll sing you a song my Grandma Shark used to sing to me when I couldn't sleep."

Grandma Shark's beautiful, soft voice filled the room, and Baby Shark's eyes got a little heavier.

"I heard there was a little shark in here who couldn't sleep," said Grandpa Shark as he swam over to Baby Shark's bed. "I know exactly what to do."

So Grandma Shark quietly swam away as Grandpa Shark took out Baby Shark's favorite bedtime story. It was about a pirate and his lost treasure. As Grandpa Shark began to read, Baby Shark felt his eyes get heavier and heavier, until . . .

Baby Shark had finally fallen asleep. Grandpa Shark tucked him in and quietly crept out to let the tired little shark sleep.

Breathing deeply, Baby Shark's mind drifted off to dreamland. Baby Shark dreamed about playing hide-and-seek with Baby Turtle and William. In his dream, he had found the perfect hiding spot!

Not only did Baby Shark dream about playing with his friends, but he also dreamed about his family. He dreamed about having a day at the beach with them.

Mostly, Baby Shark dreamed about what a great day tomorrow would be.

"What a sweet shark," Mommy Shark whispered as she watched Baby Shark sleep along with Daddy Shark, Grandma Shark, and Grandpa Shark. "I hope he is having good dreams."

Daddy Shark smiled. "Now we can all finally go to bed."